Once Tiny Always Strong

Nicole C. Follmeyer

ISBN: 9798567860533

DEDICATION

This book is dedicated to our miracle baby, Bryson Cole Follmeyer, to whom this book is about.
Born weighing 0 lbs. 14 3/4 oz. and 10 1/4 in. long, he was considered a micro preemie. No parent dreams about, thinks about, or really knows what a NICU journey is until you have no choice but to experience it. Just remember…all of this is to benefit and help your baby fight their way through the NICU. Stay positive and pray. No baby wants to fight this battle, but sometimes there is no choice.

CONTENTS

ACKNOWLEDGMENTS

Thank you to my amazing husband. I couldn't have made it through this journey without you. From the beginning, you have shown me what a perfect, supportive, loving and hard-working husband and dad you are. Thank you to all our family and friends who helped us stay positive and gave unending support. A special thanks to my parents and siblings who were always there for us. A huge thank you to all the NICU team at Holy Cross Hospital in Silver Spring, MD. We couldn't have done it without you. We are so blessed to have all the prayers and love that we received throughout this journey and onward.

* 95 days behind me and a whole lifetime in front of me *

In Loving Memory of one of our NICU Nurses
Winetta Hodges Moses
February 8, 1977 - November 9, 2020
#TEAMNETTA

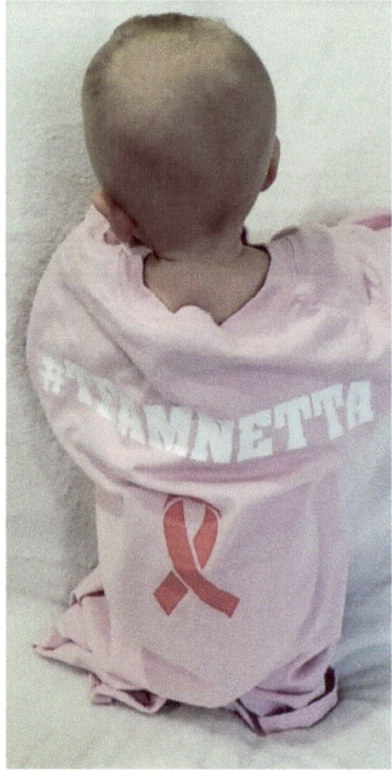

OUR JOURNEY

My husband Brian and I, got married on July 7, 2018. The following year we talked about starting a family. We never really knew how hard it could be for some people to get pregnant or that some people can't get pregnant at all. Fortunately, we were blessed and were able to get pregnant right away. We were so excited and we needed a happy moment in our life because we recently lost our first fur baby, Inari. I decided to tell Brian in a photo shoot. We both stood back to back and my sign said, "You're gong to be a Daddy" and his sign was blank. We were told to write something you love about one another. Obviously I knew what we were doing, but Brian had no clue. When we turned around to show each other what our signs said, he was shocked. He wasn't expecting that at all. And to throw him off, a few days before we had photos done, I told him I took a test and it was negative (which was actually true but I just took the test too early). We started to find fun and creative ways to tell our family and friends. It was exciting to see everyone's reactions.

As a couple weeks went by, things seem to have been going pretty smoothly. I had to adjust to doctors appointments and getting blood drawn. Then, at 12 weeks, my doctor sent me to the emergency room at Holy Cross Hospital because my blood pressure was out of control (228/155). I felt just fine and I was so upset because I was not planning on going to or staying in the hospital for any time at all. I ended up having to stay there for three days. Fortunately, after that bump in the road, things went back to kind of normal. Unfortunately, I had many things that come with pregnancy start to happen. I had a stuffy nose all the time, my feet were so swollen (from the blood pressure medicine) that I could barely walk on them, and I had to go to more doctors appointments as well as cardiologist appointments to keep an eye on my blood pressure throughout the pregnancy. On September 7, 2019, we had a gender reveal party. My sister had the results because Brian and I wanted to be surprised. She made a dozen hard boiled eggs, but one egg not hard boiled. Six were blue and six were pink. We cracked them against our foreheads, which wasn't the best idea since it hurt, to see which one was all yolk. Sure enough after we were did four each, the fifth one we both hit on our heads gave us the answer. I had pink and Brian had blue. Brian's broke and "It's a boy!"

At our 20 week ultrasound (on Friday the 13th of September), we didn't get the news we were hoping for. This is when our world turned upside down. Life instantly got harder and pregnancy got more depressing. It was hard to stay excited and happy about pregnancy when we didn't know if we were going to have our baby in the end.

So here is how it all began…

PREGNANCY

Pregnancy isn't a given…it's a gift. Fast forward to before our miracle was born. I never thought pregnancy could be so tough and scary. I was the one who thought, "How hard can it be? I just have to get through delivery. That is the hardest part, right?"…WRONG. What I didn't realize is how every day, every appointment, and every moment is a blessing. To hear your baby's heartbeat, see your baby in the sonogram, and know that they are growing and healthy is a blessing.

We had our gender reveal and the following week, I was 20 weeks. My husband and I went in for our routine sonogram, so excited to see our baby. Never did I think we would get the news we got. The doctor said, "Your baby isn't growing", "You need to go right onto bedrest", "No more working", "You will eventually be going on bedrest in the hospital until you deliver", "You will have a c-section and will most likely only be able to have c-sections for any future births", "You must deliver at Holy Cross Hospital in Silver Spring, not Germantown", "Your baby is only getting minimal blood flow from the umbilical cord and is not getting enough nutrients from the placenta to grow". With the amount of bad news we received it was like rapid fire. The doctor said, "Basically, your placenta is like a car engine. It's a bad motor and it's not giving the car what it needs to work properly. I instantly broke down in tears so many thoughts were running through my head. All I could think was, "Was it my fault? What did I do wrong? Why me?". We asked as many questions as we could think of with being very new to understanding pregnancy in itself, let alone this dilemma. Fortunately, nothing we did caused this to happen. Unfortunately, there was no way to fix it.

These are the cards God had dealt to us and we had no choice but to deal with it. From this point forward, we had two choices. We would stay positive and pray for the best or we would give up and dwell on the negative. After many depressing days, we knew that we were going to stay positive, pray, and fight for our baby.

As time went on, many things that you would normally look forward to when you are pregnant I was unable to do. Unfortunately, due to the situation we had, there was no maternity pictures, no big baby bump, no seeing the baby kick inside, and no one knowing what the outcome of our baby would be. Appointment after appointment, at least two a week, and still no changes in our baby's weight or length. At my 24 week appointment, my doctor told me, "You need to be admitted to the hospital on bedrest now" and "Every appointment I was just hoping to hear a heartbeat". I couldn't believe this was happening. It was so upsetting because not only was I going into the hospital (one of my biggest fears and a place no one wants to be), but I was going in there for good until it was time for our baby to be delivered. I got admitted on October 9, 2019 and my due date wasn't until January 27, 2020. I was devastated and so scared. It felt like the end of the world. No holidays with family, no going to family and friends events, no hanging out at home in peace and quiet. Just stuck here in the hospital, staring at the same four walls and not allowed out of the room at all. It was so hard to stay positive throughout this process. My husband told me, "No matter what, we are in this together and I will be here with you every day and night." I had suitcases packed for a three month stay. I felt like I was never going to go home. All we would hear is, "High Risk (HRP)", "Long-Term Patient", "Room 3203". Thinking every day would be a nightmare, I was proven wrong. It wasn't my favorite place to be, but I was there to save my baby. The nurses that took care of me were amazing and so nice. That made it so much easier to be there. The two biggest reasons for me being in the hospital on bedrest were to get a lot of protein and have no stress. In order to make this happen the doctors kept the IV out and let me give blood every three days instead since I am terrified of needles. Every nurse who was assigned to me, helped me with getting blood taken. Whether it was holding my hand, numbing my arm, distracting me, or even hugging me; it all worked. There were two beta shots that I was unable to turn down. These shots would help the baby's lungs. Things happen for a reason. My baby saved my life because by getting pregnant with him, we were able to catch my high blood pressure of 228/155 at 12 weeks of pregnancy, and now it was my turn to save his life.

As time went on, many thoughts were running through my head…"Why me?" "Why us?" "Why him". Finally, we had a family friend who shared the story of her baby girl who was a preemie. She shared that yes, it is scary and not in anyone's plan, but the power of prayer is stronger than fear. I did my best to take as much advice as I could and to stay strong and positive throughout this journey.

I kept busy by doing word searches, crafts, and having my family visit me. When my husband and family were there, it felt like just another day; but when my family went to leave, I just wanted to go home.

As time and days passed, being at the hospital became a routine. Not saying it was easy, but I managed. My mom would come switch out with my husband when he had to go to work and she stayed with me until he got off. One of the nurses said, "I know this may seem like a huge part of your life/time wasted, but once this is all over, it will seem like it was so short. Only three months out of your entire lifetime". I will never forget that. She was right. I never thought that I would make friends from being stuck in a hospital room, but many of the nurses became my friends and hospital family. Being a longterm patient was scary, but it made me the stronger person I am today.

"You were given this life because you are strong enough
to live it"
-Unknown

PREPARATION

Every day being told, "This is what will happen if you baby lives and this is what will happen if your baby doesn't make it", was devastating. This was one of the hardest things to hear. The doctors told us that 500 grams was the weight for a baby to be viable. So that is what we prayed for.

Unfortunately our little boy was not at the 500 gram mark, and they had no choice but to take him and have the NICU team do whatever they could to help him grow outside of my belly. At this time, it was all in God's hands. All we could do is pray for a miracle.

And sure enough, that's what we got…A MIRACLE.

REVERSAL

On October 22nd at 9:00 p.m., our nightmare began. The nurses were not able to find the baby's heartbeat. Nurse after nurse came in trying to find it, but no luck. He was small so it was already so hard to find, but usually these nurses could find it right away. Finally, after four nurses tried, they got it. His heartbeat kept going up and down on the belly band and it was not looking good. Everyday at the hospital appointments, the word we never wanted to hear was "reversal". After doing a sonogram that night, we were told they saw reversal. This means it will be an emergency c-section and they need to get the baby out as soon as they can. My room immediately flooded with doctors and nurses. I was terrified and felt completely out of control. I looked at my husband and without hesitation told him to call my parents.

I was instantly put on magnesium to help with our baby's brain development. I was monitored every 15 minutes and had to stay on the belly band until the next morning. I was told when my doctor arrives, I will be taken in for a c-section. Around 9:00 a.m., Dr. Ashkin walked in and said, "It's time". I was so terrified that myself and the baby weren't going to make it. My parents said they will be waiting for me when I come out. As I was getting wheeled to the operating room, my dad said, "Those are both of my babies in there. Please make sure they will be good." The doctor replied, "Your big baby will be just fine, but I don't know about the little one." I couldn't even think straight. I was taken in to get a spinal tap. I was crying and couldn't believe this was happening Then a woman said, "Hi Nicole, do you remember me? I am your best friend's mom's friend." She was amazing and she kept my mind off what was happening at the moment. She talked to me about my wedding, my friend's wedding, and the cakes I make. What was a blessing in disguise, was that she only works at that hospital once a month and the day I was delivering happened to be the one day she worked there. Next thing you know, I was being flipped onto the operating table. I was given a lemon swab before I went in and I was still clenching onto it in the operating room. My husband said, "I am so proud of you", with tears in his eyes. My doctor began and there was a lot of a tugging and pulling feel (just like my mom told me it would feel like). Brian kept me distracted by talking about what name we were going to give our little boy. We decided on Bryson Cole Follmeyer. A little bit of Brian's name (Bri) and a little bit of my name, Nicole (Cole). My doctor said, "You're doing good kid."

We were waiting to hear our baby cry, but there was no cry. Then my doctor said, "Happy Birthday" at 9:24 a.m. Surprisingly, our son came out breathing on his own. He was not at all what any parent would be expecting to see; a little tiny baby wrapped in plastic and swaddled in a blanket. Love at first sight. They quickly showed me Bryson and rushed him into the NICU. From there, we headed to recovery.

You always hear about how you will get to hold you baby right away and that it's the best feeling in the world. We didn't get that opportunity due to his situation, but fortunately, our baby boy came out alive and breathing. Weighing only 417 grams, which is 0 lbs 14 3/4 oz and 10 1/4 inches long and which was more than what the ultrasound read at 386 grams, his NICU battle began.

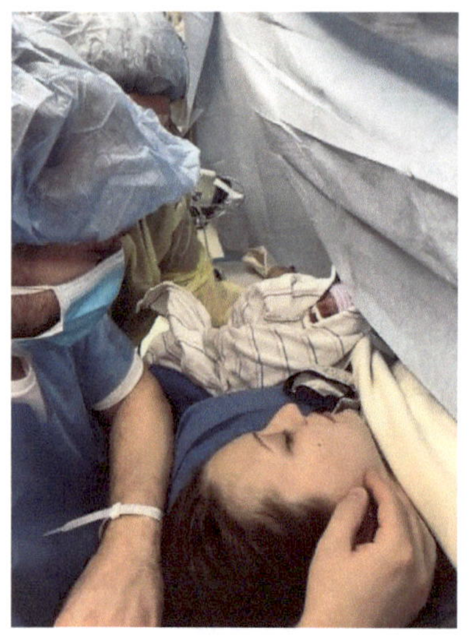
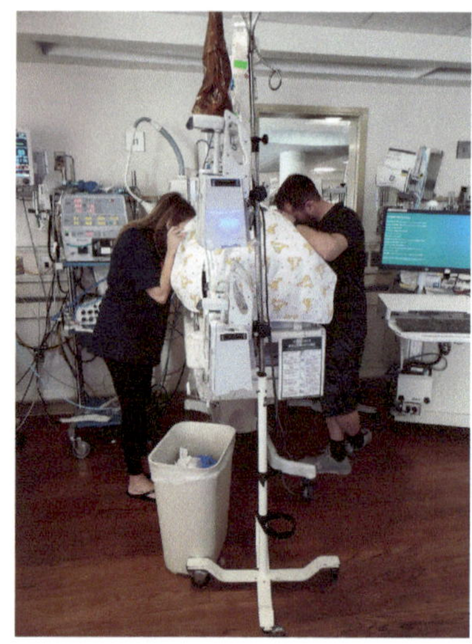

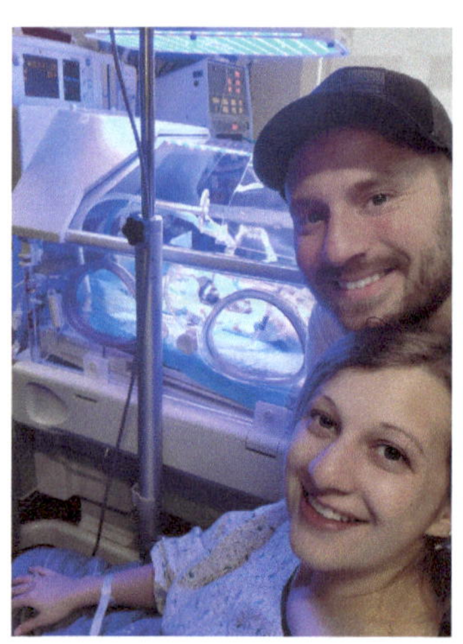
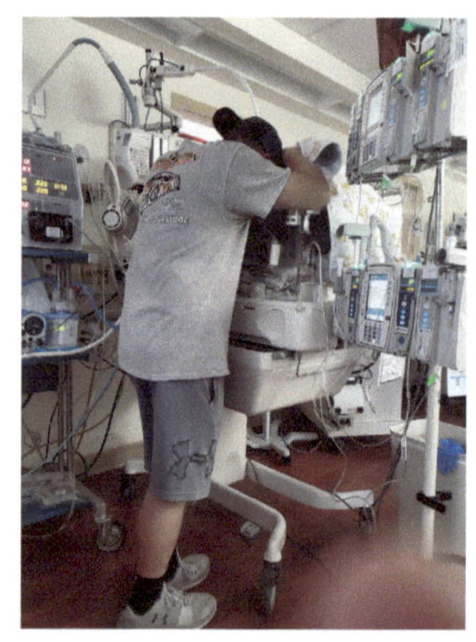

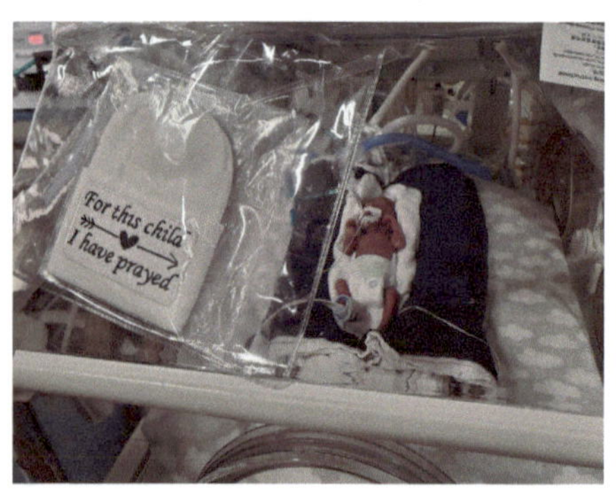
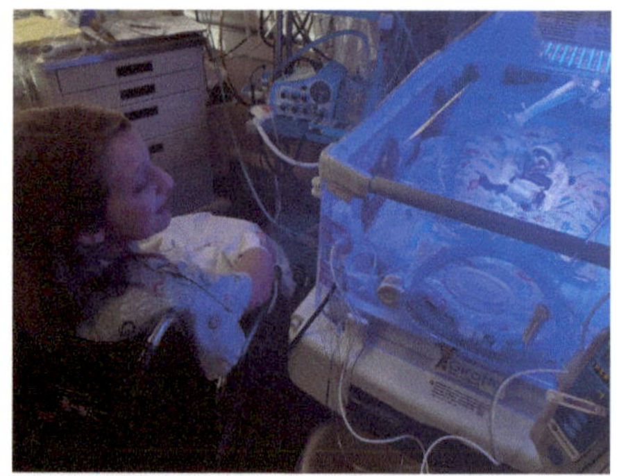

LEARNING THE NICU

Time in the NICU…
Each second feels like minutes.
Each minute feels like hours.
Each hour feels like days.

NICU - Neonatal Intensive Care Unit
Where to begin…
No parent wants to leave the hospital, when discharged, without your baby. At first I cried. I was terrified. Then, I saw you. You were my baby. You just came sooner then we had planned. But it was in God's plan. "Micro prematurity", they said. "NICU", they said. Everything was so different, but what hadn't changed is that you were still my baby and I was still your mommy. If you could do this, so could I. Seeing you all hooked up, under the blue jaundice light, no clothes, in an incubator, leads on your belly was a terrifying sight to see. I never knew a baby could be so small. Becoming a new parent and I couldn't even touch or hold you. In the beginning, it was heartbreaking to have to learn to trust the NICU while we couldn't be there or when we had to go home. After becoming more educated on the NICU, we started to have a NICU family. The NICU, doctors, nurses, and equipment are not what you expect as a new parent, but now they are part of you and your baby's lives. All of these overwhelming things are here to help your baby. These NICU moments are yours to experience and to share when you are ready. The NICU staff had questions from us constantly and they answered every one with detail; explaining what could happen or what will happen. Every day we would get updates either in person

or in a detailed phone call. Information and words you have never heard of became our new vocabulary. Hearing grams instead of ounces or pounds became our normal. Every day we were praying for the best update we could hope for. Always praying for weight gaining and never weight loss. Praying for no brain bleeds, infections, sickness, eye sight problems, or lung development issues. Just praying for our baby boy to be healthy. Every day was a roller coaster with ups and downs. The first week they told us is always the "Honeymoon Stage". Following that is when the roller coaster ride begins. We were always asking questions like, "Have you seen a baby this small survive?" The NICU team always giving us positive thoughts and explaining how they will do everything they can to help our little boy. That special feeling of holding their tiny hand, changing their tiny diaper and having it weighed, taking their temperature, or even just watching them breathe; all these moments are so important to your little baby fighting their way through. The NICU has happy moments and sad moments. Every baby's journey is different when it comes to their health. Some preemies are stronger than others, and some need care 24/7. But they are all fighting for their life in the NICU to go to their forever home.

Finally, three weeks later, Bryson's NICU nurse asked me, "Do you want to kangaroo today?". I couldn't believe it! I was going to hold my baby for the first time. Even with all the wires, leads (that didn't like sticking to his skin), and being hooked up to "the jet" (machine to help him breathe) it was an unbelievable feeling. He was so fragile and small, and I was just praying he would fight through it all.

Many times during the journey in the NICU, your baby will take one step forward and two steps back. You sit there and watch them breathe, sleep, and fight for their life.

Nourish them with everything you can. Don't be afraid and always talk to them. Your baby hears you and they feel when you are there.

I'm not going to sugar coat it; the NICU journey is HARD. The wires, tubes, and beeps from the monitors are so overwhelming at first. Always hoping for no "Bradys" (which means set the alarms off). But then you start to learn what they are for and how they are helping your baby or babies. You start to get used to them. During the NICU journey, there are days of happiness, days of sadness and days of guilt. But if it wasn't for the NICU, our babies wouldn't be here. We are so blessed to have had this amazing care. Our awesome care came from Holy Cross Hospital NICU in Silver Spring, MD.

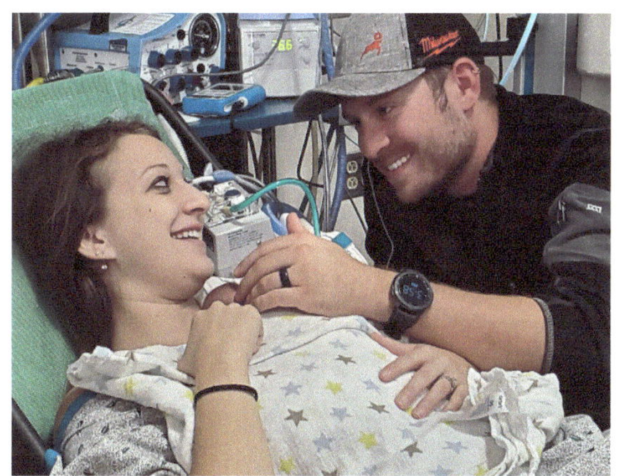

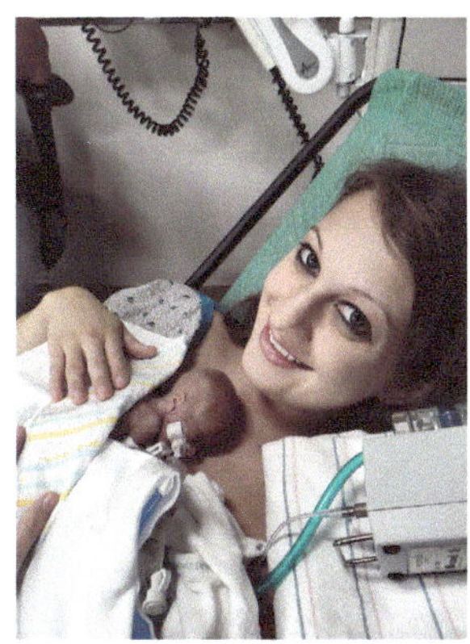
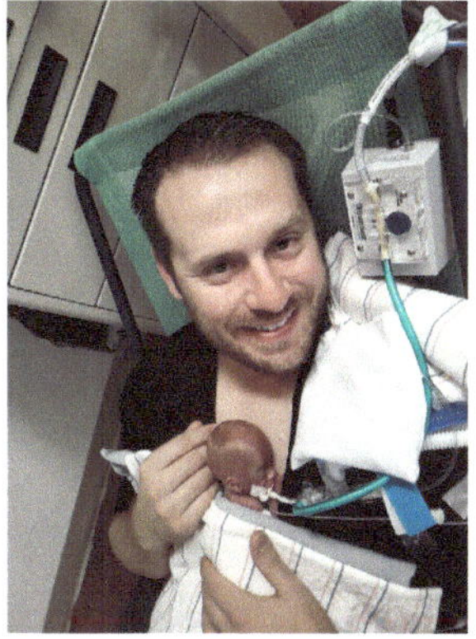
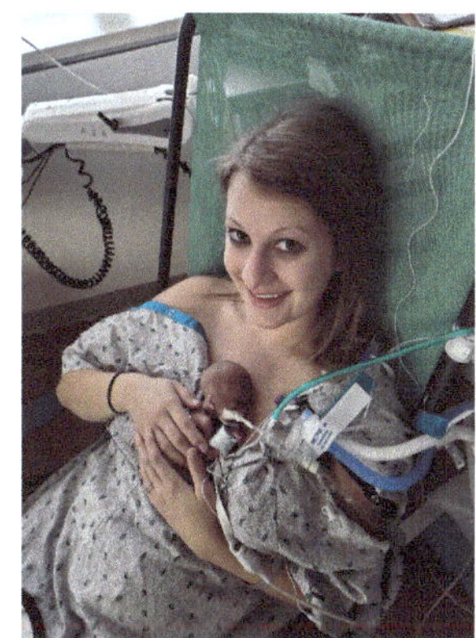

THE POWER OF PRAYER

Every day pray! Even if you don't think it will work or don't believe in it. Trust me, from someone who experienced the power of prayer first hand, it works. It doesn't matter where you are, what time it is, or what you believe in…just pray. My husband never really prayed, but when our situation happened with Bryson, things changed. I found my husband praying. Praying for a miracle to help our baby survive and fight the battle. It was an amazing thing to see how prayer worked. God still worked his power of prayer. Every day at the NICU I wore my sweatshirt that says, "God has my back" because I knew he always does. Once our family and friends were informed about Bryson's situation, I would get texts, calls, and/or emails saying we are praying for Bryson and your family. How amazing it was to see that all these prayers were for our little man and how powerful they were. Whenever you think you are going to give up, don't. Just pray.

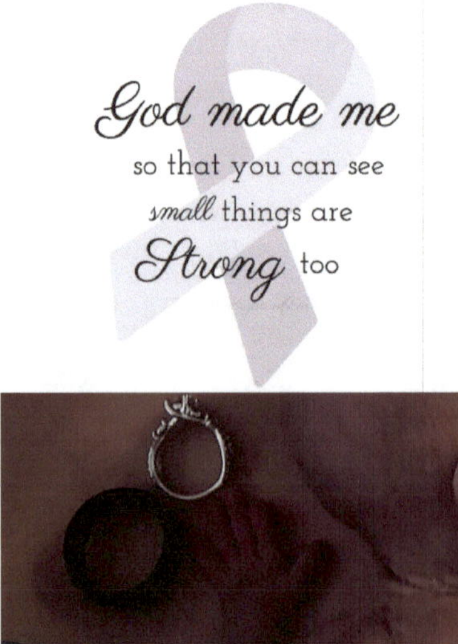

OVERWHELMED

A journey in the NICU is overwhelming, there is no doubt about that. It is stressful and hard to watch your baby fight for their life. The only thing you can do as a parent is pray and let your baby know that you are there fighting this battle with them. There is so many ups and downs and sometimes you just want to cry. There is so many words that you have never heard of before and don't understand that you do more research than you ever have. There were so many days that I was so exhausted mentally and physically that I just wanted to give up. But I knew no matter what, I needed to push myself through and fight for Bryson just like he was fighting for himself. He was going through more than I have ever been through in my lifetime and he hasn't even been able to live his life yet. He truly is a fighter. Seeing our son go through all of this has made us strong as parents. There is a saying, "The only person as strong as a preemie is their parents". Well isn't that the truth. You are battling this fight as a family and you will do anything for them to survive. We drove every day one hour to and one hour back from the hospital just to spend as much time as we could with Bryson. I would go up in the morning and spend all day there until the NICU had their shift change at 6:30 p.m. From 6:30 a.m to 7:30 a.m. and from 6:30 p.m. and 7:30 p.m., the NICU closed so they could shift change and give the next nurse all of the information and updates about your baby. My husband would come up after work to spend the rest of the day with our son.

The best thing we had was having a primary for our baby. A primary nurse is a NICU nurse who is assigned to your baby whenever they work, unless there is a specific reason they can't. Our NICU primary nurse was amazing. She always kept us updated. She would always make sure we understood everything and answered all our questions. We would receive adorable pictures of moments we couldn't be there to capture from her. If I had any questions or concerns throughout the night or even in the middle of the night, she would answer. Every ounce was a miracle so anytime there was weight gain, she made sure we would know right away. Many parents plan to have monthly milestone pictures and first holiday pictures when having a baby. I was devastated when I thought I would miss these opportunities because Bryson had to be in the NICU. I had no need to be upset because our NICU nurse helped us capture all of these moments and got awesome pictures. Having her made this journey a little less overwhelming and she always made us feel comfortable. Not only did we have an amazing NICU nurse watching over our little man; we gained a great friend. We love you, Erin.

The doctors updated us every day on Bryson. If we were there and the doctors came by the bedside, they would give us any information in person and always asked, "So what questions do you have for me?" It was so nice to be able to ask questions or state concerns and have them be able to tell us the answers right away. All the doctors were amazing and so helpful. If we weren't there at the time the doctors came around, they would call us or leave us a detailed message and if we had questions, we could call them back. We were so blessed to have our baby boy in the hands of this amazing NICU.

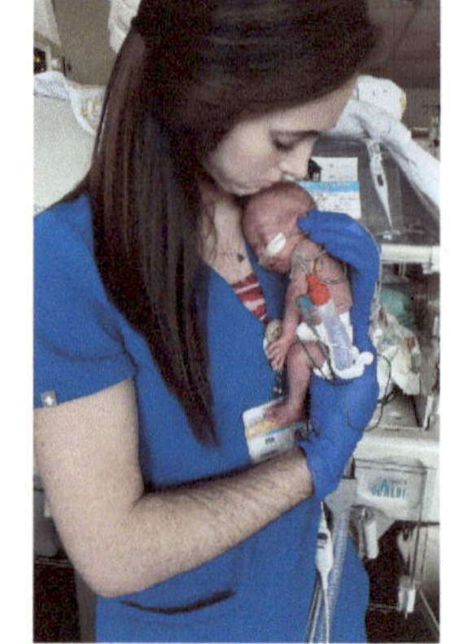

LIFE IN THE NICU

Life in the NICU. It's not the plan or choice for anyone. But if this is what you have to conquer, it is not impossible. Instead of watching your baby grow on sonograms inside of your belly, you get to watch your baby grow on the outside. The NICU room becomes your "body on the outside". I learned a new appreciation for life and this journey has not only made me a better person but a better mother.

Bryson was born weighing only 0 lbs 14 3/4 oz (417 grams) and 10 1/4 in long. He was born at 26 weeks and he was the size of a hand. His skin was see through and he looked more like a baby bird than a human baby. We were told that he was the smallest and sickest baby in the NICU. Not what anyone wants to hear. But we were told to trust in all the NICU doctors and nurses because this is what they do every day. As new parents or anyone who is new as a NICU parent, here is what you can expect.

What to expect:

Let's start by saying "Nano Preemie" and "Micro Preemie" diapers. Yes, you read that correctly. I couldn't believe a diaper could be so tiny. It was smaller then a baby doll's diaper. I didn't even know there was a such thing. The NICU was so sweet and let us have one to keep.

There are many things that you will see, hear, and learn about while being in the NICU. Because your baby didn't get the time inside you to fully form, some things our babies will have to do differently or have done to them due to being born early. Here are most of them: Jaundice, IVs, Pic Line, Heel Pricks, Blood Transfusions, Eye Appointments, Brain Scans, Heart Ultrasounds, Feeding

Tubes, Incubator, The Jet, CPAP, SIPAP, Hi-Flow, Oxygen, Monitors, Brady, Hi-Setting, Reflux, and Leads.

Anytime the NICU nurses or doctors ask you, "Do you want to do hands on?" Always say Yes! Your baby knows you and they can feel when you interact with them, even if it's just to change their diaper.

Your baby will have a feeding tube for most of the time they are in the NICU until they can take all of their milk through a bottle. It will be through their mouth and then eventually through their nose.

Incubator - Seeing our baby through this closed in bed was so hard. To not be able to touch my baby and only be able to look through the glass of the incubator. Eventually, we were able to touch our baby through the little incubator windows. An incubator provides an environment that can be adjusted to provide the ideal temperature as well as the perfect amount of oxygen, humidity, and light. Basically, it creates the inside of a Mommy to help a baby survive outside of the womb. Bryson was in an incubator for two months. After that, he went into an open crib in the NICU.

"The Jet" - This is a huge ventilation contraption. It usually is on babies smaller then 1 lb. and it only has a half an inch of movement of the tube to help him breathe. You could see his chest jetting, which this is scary to watch. If the tube came out of that half an inch section and you can hear him cry, it was not a good thing. This would mean that "The Jet" wasn't in the correct placement to support Bryson's breathing. Bryson liked to test his nurses and pull his tubes out. His arms wouldn't stop moving and he always grabbed onto the tubes and equipment. When I kangarooed for the first time, Bryson was on the jet. He decided he wanted to look the opposite way of how the nurse placed his head due to being hooked up to the jet. He started to turn his head and all the nurses ran quickly to stop him from turning because he would pull the tube for the jet out of its placement. Bryson was in this stage for about three weeks.

"SI-PAP" (Synchronized Inspiratory Positive Airway Pressure) - Even though this was the second stage, it looked worse. The NICU warned us that this step looks worse but that it is a good step forward. At this stage, his face was covered by a soft helmet and a chin strap with oxygen attached to it. Every three hours, the nurses would take it off to massage his head. Because his bones were not formed all the way, they basically dented and squished. Bryson was in an extra small size helmet and nose piece. SIPAP can provide more support, similar to ventilation. Bryson was on this stage for about one week.

"C-PAP" (Continuous Positive Airway Pressure) - This stage looks very similar to SI-PAP. C-PAP is used to deliver constant air pressure into the baby's nose. This helps the air sacs in the lungs stay open and helps prevent apnea. Bryson was on this stage for about one and a half weeks.

"Hi-Flow Nasal Cannula" (HFNC) - This was the best stage of them all. We could finally see our little boy's face. This stage has prongs that go in their nose and they get oxygen through that. This stage is a "non-invasive" respiratory support. Hi-Flow has a good amount of room for movement. Bryson was on this stage for about seven weeks.

Throughout this journey, there will be many scares. Bryson definitely gave us many. One specific scare was when I was learning to bottle feed him for the first time. I had just started and he took his first two gulps and it went "down the wrong pipe". But because he is a baby, he didn't know how to cough it up. I was patting his back trying to get him to breathe, but then he turned blue. Calmly, our NICU nurse said, "I am going to take him." She instantly jumped into action. More nurses and the respiratory therapist came over to assist. I was terrified and was crying. There were nurses that were comforting me while everything was happening. Finally, he let out a cry. They said, "Hear that, he's back". I was so thankful they took action. They will forever be our superheroes. They saved Bryson's life.

Finally, with about ten days left in the NICU, Bryson was able to use "Hi-Flow" just for feedings. He needed the extra oxygen support when he drank a bottle, but otherwise, he was doing great.

On January 22, 2020, Bryson's doctor said it was time to take the feeding tube out and get a car seat test, CPR class, discharge class, speak to the nutritionist about feeds, and almost the day to take our baby home. We were prepping to bring Bryson home. The NICU is awesome at helping you know what appointments to make. They set up your first outpatient appointments and they teach you all of the information that you would need to know. Being a NICU parent has taught me many things and has guided me through being a first time parent. I am forever grateful for all of the help the NICU has given us.

Every milestone in the NICU is a moment to celebrate. Whether its gaining one ounce, taking a bottle, first time kangarooing, bonding, moving from incubator to crib, or any other important moments; make sure you write them down, journal them, take pictures and keep track of your NICU journey. Keep track of all the daily positives and the daily challenges. Make sure you always write down notes and/or questions for the doctors and nurses because when they ask you, "What questions do you have for us?", you will have so many thoughts going through your head and you don't want to forget anything. Every moment in the NICU is and will always be part of you and your baby. Every time you see your baby, just remember, they are a miracle.

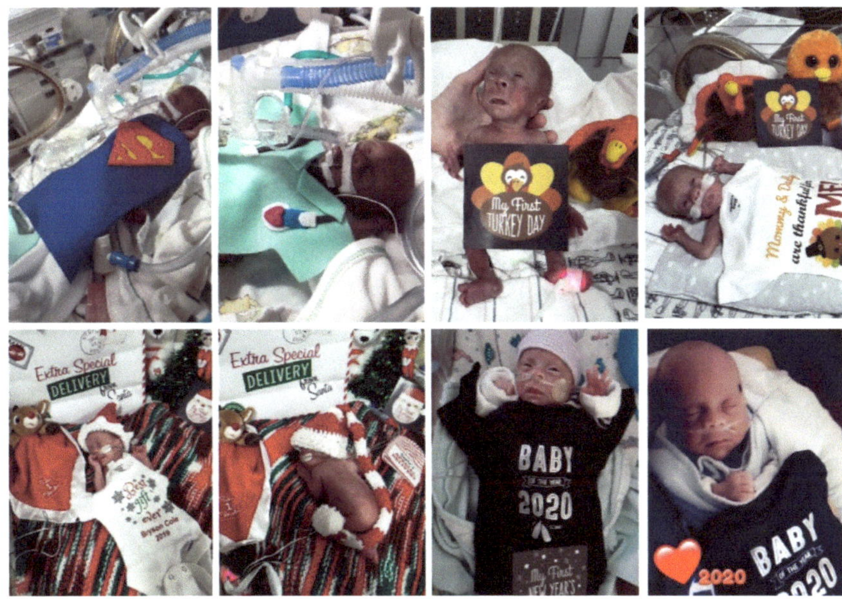

A PARENT

What does it mean to be a parent?

It means knowing that every day is a blessing and a gift. It means knowing that you are the luckiest person in the world just to be a parent. It means cherishing every moment and every breath with such intensity, that you feel tears come to your eyes for no apparent reason. But most of all, not taking any moment or second for granted.

Our miracle has shown us how to become stronger parents, prayers make miracles happen, and that God is in control.

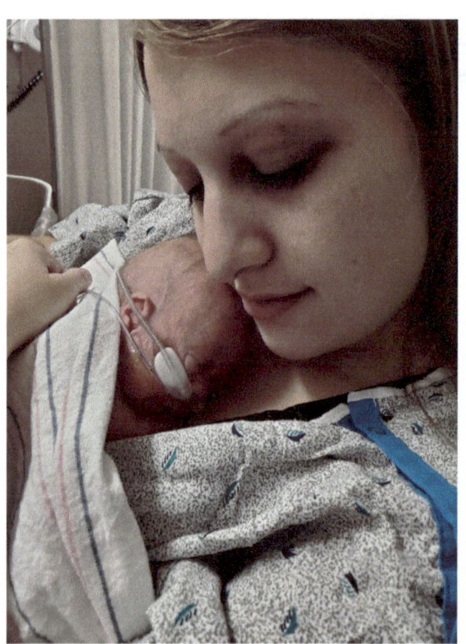

NICU GRAD

95 days in the NICU felt like a lifetime to us. All of his first holidays, monthly milestones, first baths, first bottle feeds, were all spent in the NICU. There were many days of growth and there were some days of setbacks. Once he learned to bottle feed, not rely on the feeding tube, and had no bradys, we knew we were getting closer to being able to take our little boy home. We had the car seat test, where Bryson had to sit in his car seat while hooked up to all the monitors and not brady for two hours. Once he passed that, we talked about his date to come home. Obviously, between the timing of the car seat test and the date to take him home, things could change at anytime if Bryson had any red flags. The doctors and nurses had prepped us for life at home with our baby boy. My husband and I, took the two mandatory classes in order to take him home, which were a discharge class and CPR class for infants. Then we did our in-room stay, which was our first time with Bryson alone in a room. The nurses and doctors were right around the corner just in case anything happened. Finally, on January 26, 2020 (one day before Bryson's due date), the doctor asked, "Are you ready to take him home?" I couldn't believe we were hearing those words. The words we have been waiting to hear for 95 days. The next thing you know…we had a NICU Grad! We were going HOME! Bryson spent his first three months of his life in the NICU and had never seen the outside world. It was amazing to experience his first breath of outside air. Bryson was in Room "B" in the corner. It was his home for a while so it was very different when we didn't travel to the NICU every day, bring breastmilk to the NICU, hang out in our

"corner", see the nurses and doctors, get updates, or hear the beeping and sounds of all the monitors. This was the start of Bryson's life at HOME We said goodbye to all his NICU nurses and doctors and said goodbye to his "corner", which was his home for his first 95 days of life. We did the NICU Grad Walk to every room in the NICU and we were headed home.

The NICU experience changed me. It taught me how to be stronger than I ever could have imagined. It taught me what to look forward to at home with a baby. It taught me how to appreciate the small things in life. It taught me to recognize all of the people who checked in and sat with me during a hard time. It taught me that life can always be worse so be grateful for the cards you were dealt. Most of all, it taught me my son is a fighter and every baby in the NICU is a fighter. No matter how long they are there, how big they are, how small they are, or even if they don't make it home, they are all fighters.

No one will truly understand what it is like to go through the NICU journey and understand how hard it is until you have to sit next to your baby and watch them fight for their life. My heart goes out to everyone who has been a NICU parent or is currently undergoing the NICU experience.

Bryson Cole came home on a monitor full time and oxygen only for feedings. He has no health complications. He was on a fortified diet by the NICU nutritionist, half breastmilk and half AR liquid formula. He was eating two ounces every three hours. He was on poly-vi-sol, which is a vitamin, with iron once a day. He weighed 4 lbs and 13 oz. when we brought him home. He had a inguinal hernia and a hernia in his belly button. He had hypospadias, which wouldn't be able to be fixed until he was about one year old. He had two preemie marks that most premature babies have, a "stork bite" and an "angel kiss". He will have premature lung disease until he is two years old. This all may seem like many things, but overall, he is happy and healthy with no life threatening or long term health issues.

The NICU has never and will never leave us. They are a part of our lives forever. We still hear the sounds of monitors and will never forget how tiny Bryson was. And we will never forget how the NICU saved our son!

I am proud to be a preemie parent and I know our preemies will conquer and continue to shock the world with their excellence. Together we will make a difference in the world.

On October 23, 2020, Bryson turned ONE! Yes, I couldn't even believe it. How fast the first year flew by. He is healthy and thriving. He weighs 15 lbs 1 oz and he's 25.5 inches long. He had the inguinal hernia surgery when he was about four months old and only weighed 5-6 lbs. It was terrifying considering how small he was and he had to go under anesthesia for his surgery. He did great and everything went as planned. He came off of all monitors and oxygen at about six months old. We have had many doctors appointments, of course, but everything looks great. He is growing and gaining weight, which is what we always love to hear. We still get excited when we hear how much he weighs at every appointment. He passed his hearing appointment, finally, after three different attempts. But overall, our little boy is alive and healthy and there is nothing more we could ask for.

He is OUR LITTLE MIRACLE!

Two pieces of advice if you ever have to fight the NICU battle:

1. Go in with a positive mindset and never give up. As long as you are fighting, so will your baby.
2. The power of prayer. Pray on it, pray over it, and pray through it!

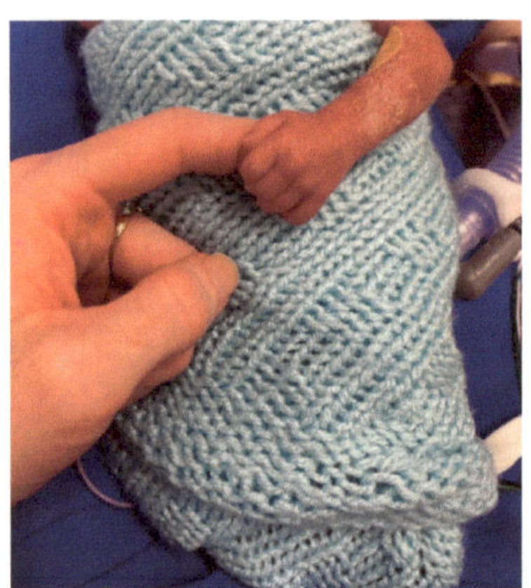

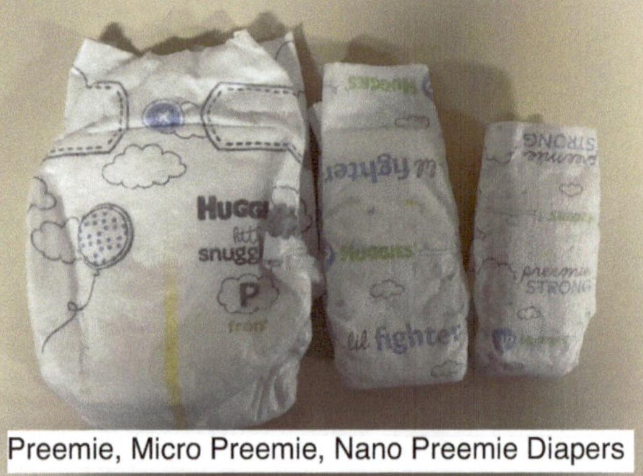
Preemie, Micro Preemie, Nano Preemie Diapers

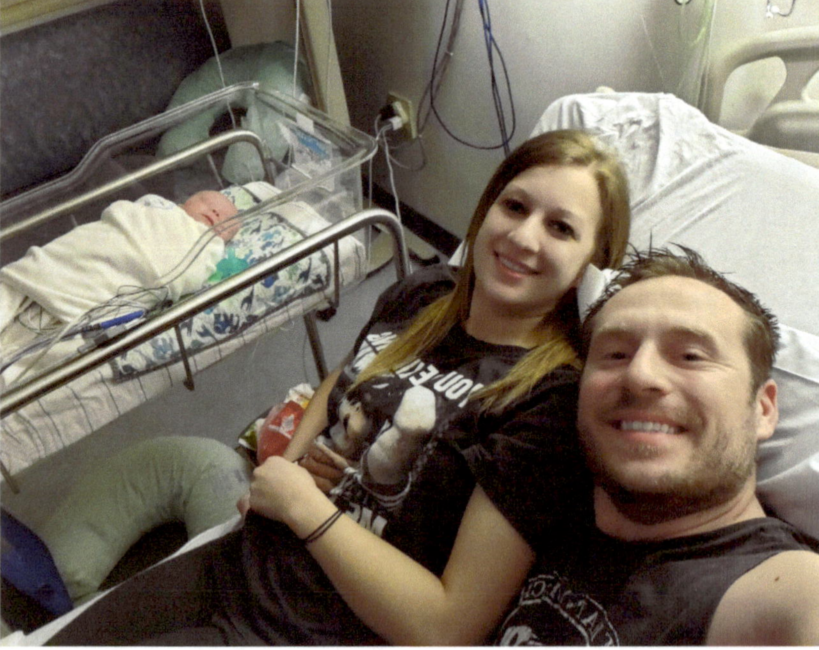

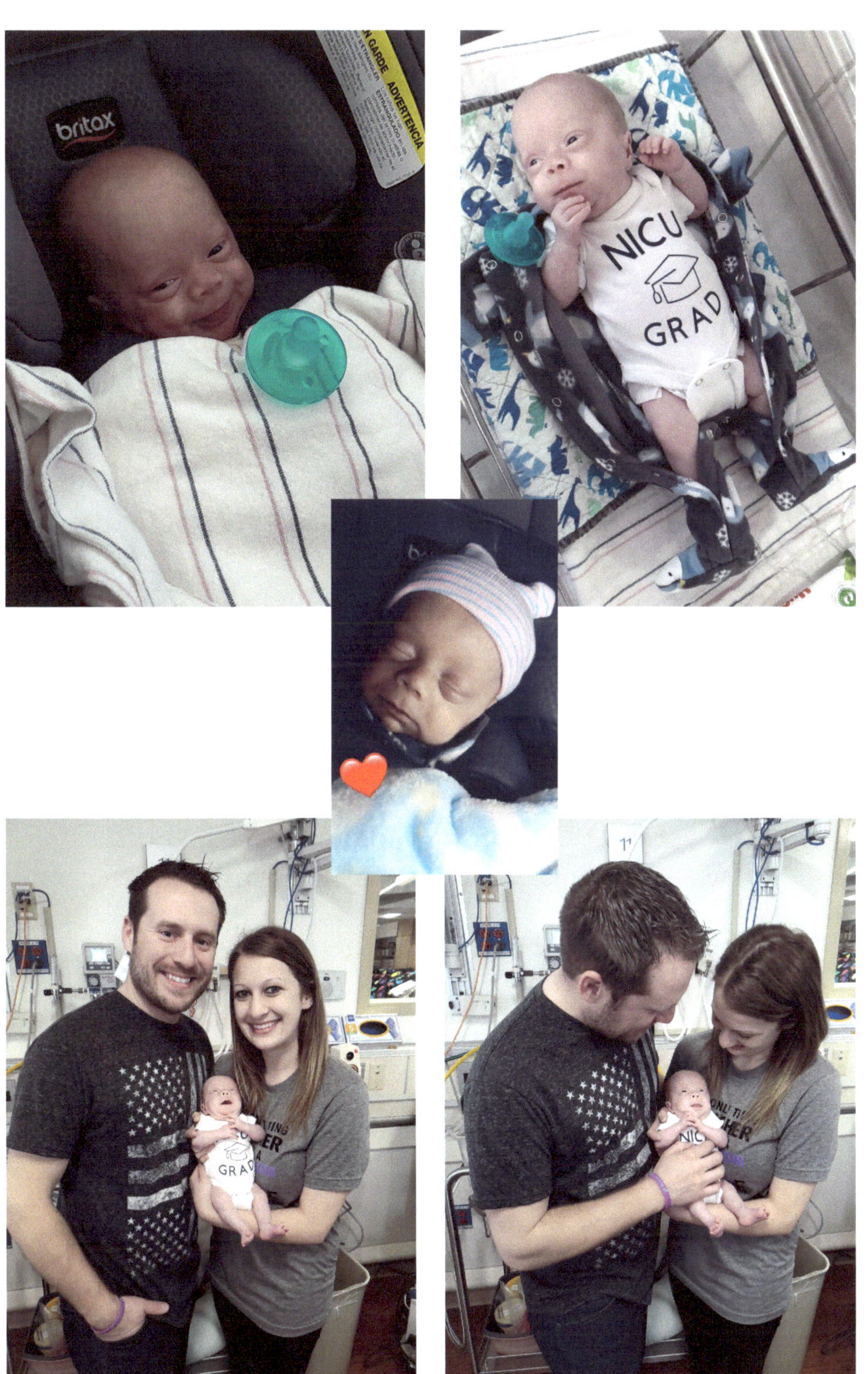

britax
NICU
GRAD

QUOTES & AWARENESS

September - NICU Awareness Month

November 17th - National Preemie Day

"Sometimes the smallest things take up the most room in your heart"
-Winnie the Pooh

"A preemie asked his mother… "Mommy, why are you always hugging me?" His mother replied, "Because I'm making up for the days I had to wait to hold you." Then he asked, "Mommy, why so many kisses?" And she replied, "i am making up for all the weeks there was glass between us." "Well Mommy, why are there sometimes tears in your eyes when you tell me you love me?" She replied, "Because I prayed so many days and nights for you. You were born very early and very small." And finally he asked, "Mommy, why was I born early?" And his Mommy replied, "Because God knew how much I needed you. You are my miracle."
-

To the NICU Team:
"A little something for your tree,
For when you see it think of me.
And how you saved my life that year,
And eased all of my parents fears.
You may not wear a cape,
Your job's not fighting crime,
But when I think of superheroes,
it's you that comes to mind."
-Unknown

Songs that helped me through this journey:

- "You are the Reason" By Calum Scott and Leona Lewis
- "Lord I Need You" By Matt Maher
- "Cornerstone By Hillsong
- "Carry Me Through" By Dave Barnes
- "Our God" By Chris Tomlin
- "Life Ain't Fair" By Canaan Smith

ABOUT THE AUTHOR

My name is Nicole Follmeyer. I was 27 years old when I became a mom to our miracle. Brian and I are so blessed to be Bryson's parents. He made our dreams and prayers come true. We believe in God, prayer, and miracles and this story will tell you why.

I was a Zumba instructor, office manager for my Dad's car business, and own my own cake business, Bake N' Time. After having Bryson and all of the complications that came with him, I ended up being a full time mom and still run my cake business. Thank you to my husband who has made this possible so I can spend all day with Bryson and not miss any more time with our little man.

Bryson's journey has inspired me to write this book to help other families know what to look forward to if they have to go through the NICU. As first time parents and having no past experience of NICU journeys in our families, we were totally blindsided. We had to learn as we went and didn't really know anyone who had this exact or similar situation.

We didn't know if it was possible to have a positive outcome out of the NICU.

I hope this book will help other families going through the NICU journey to stay strong and stay positive.

My son, Bryson Cole Follmeyer, is living proof that miracles do happen!

PICTURES THEN

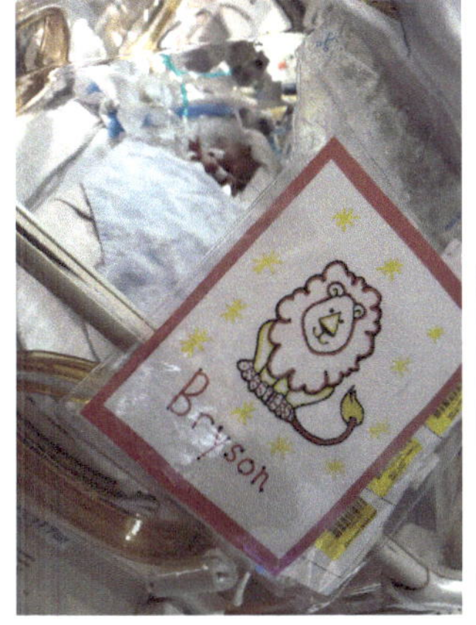
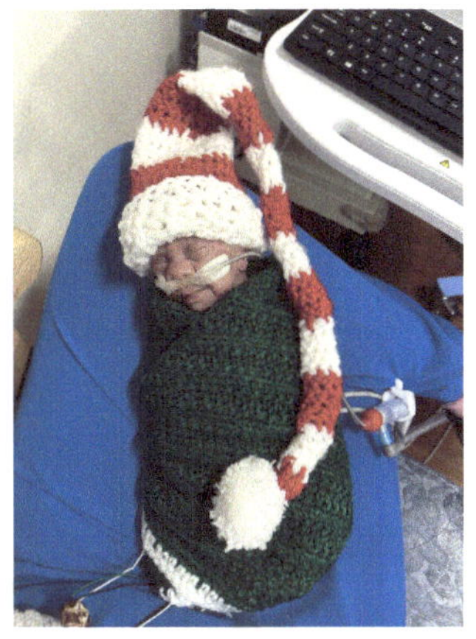
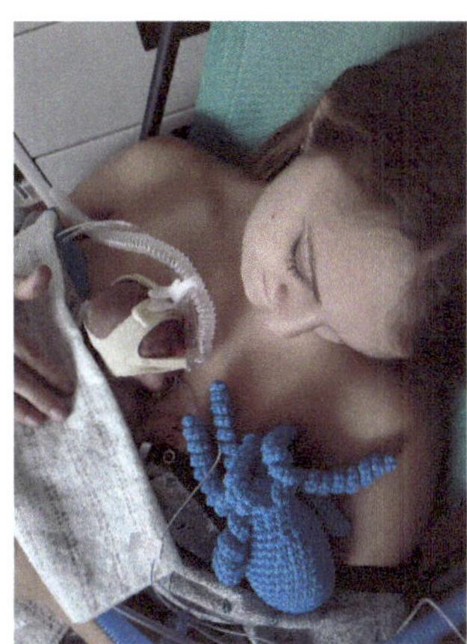
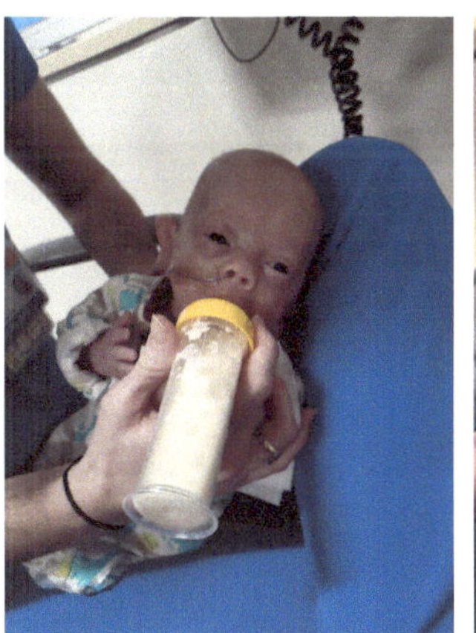
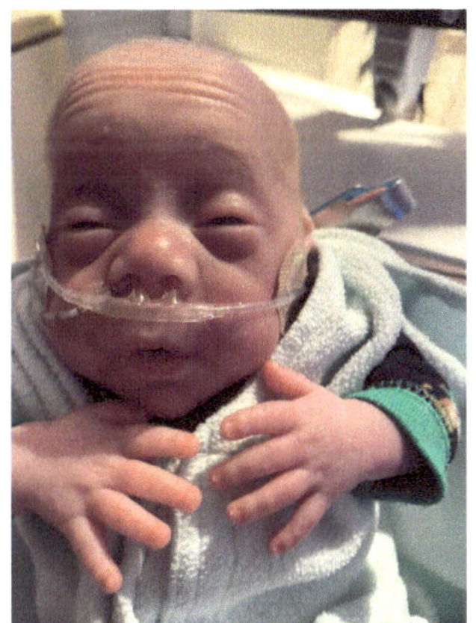

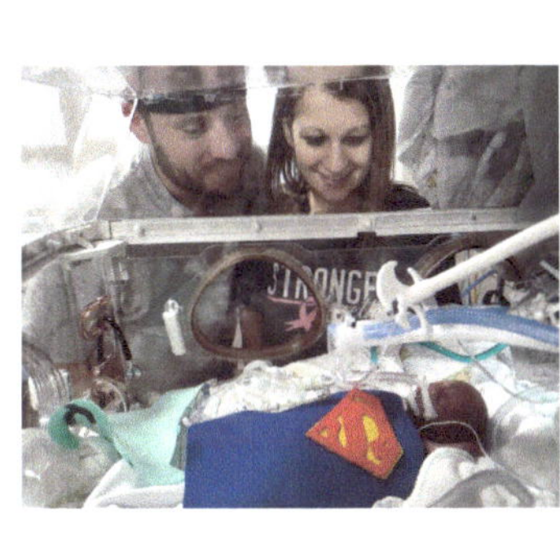
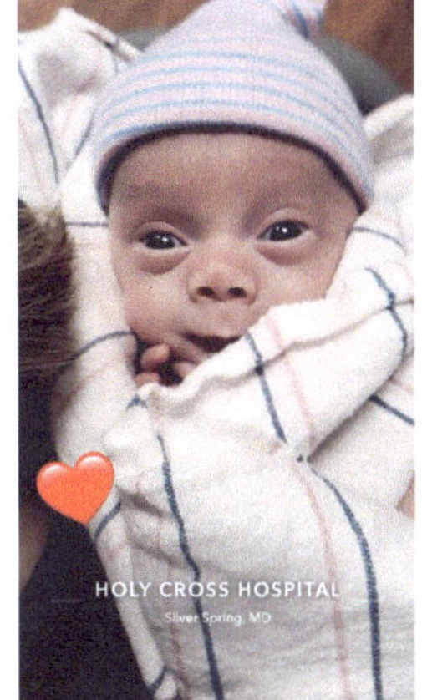
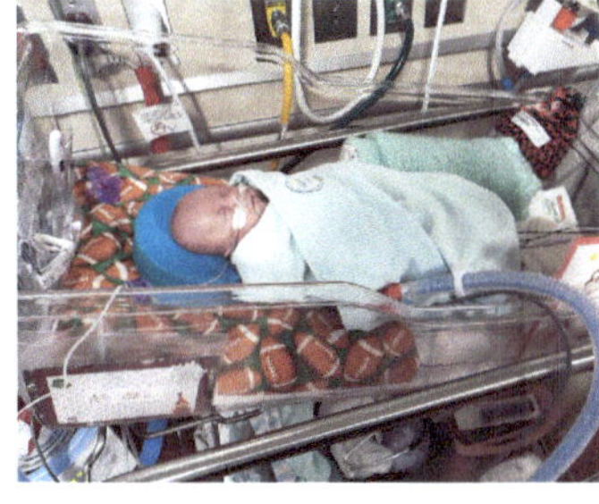

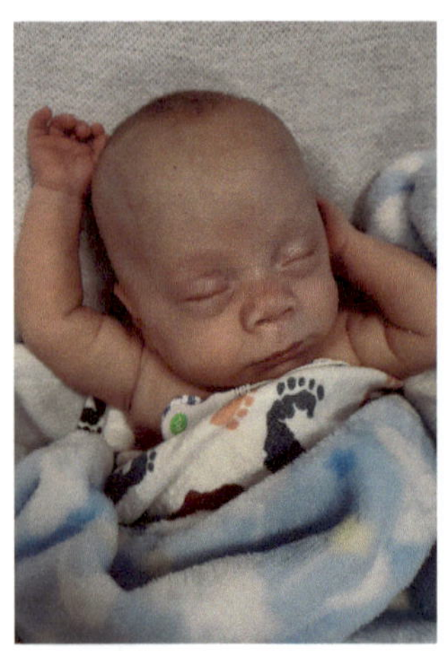
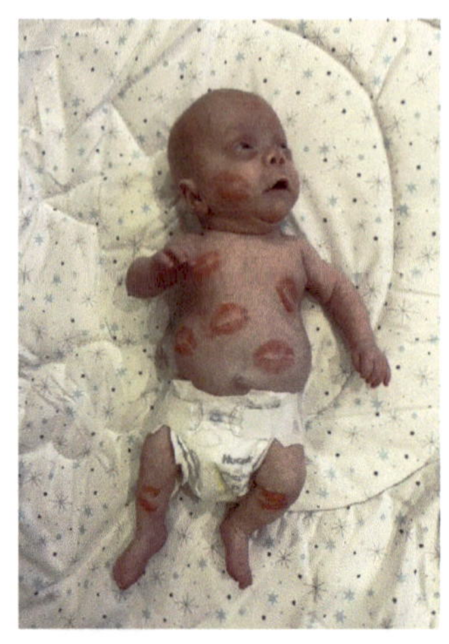

I'm
a little
Miracle
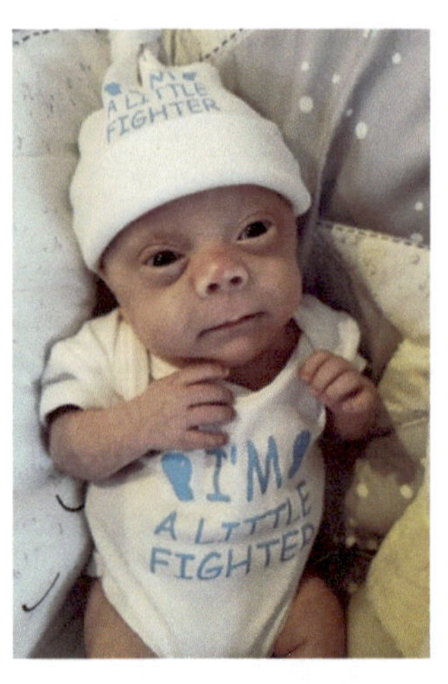
A LITTLE
FIGHTER
I'M
A LITTLE
FIGHTER
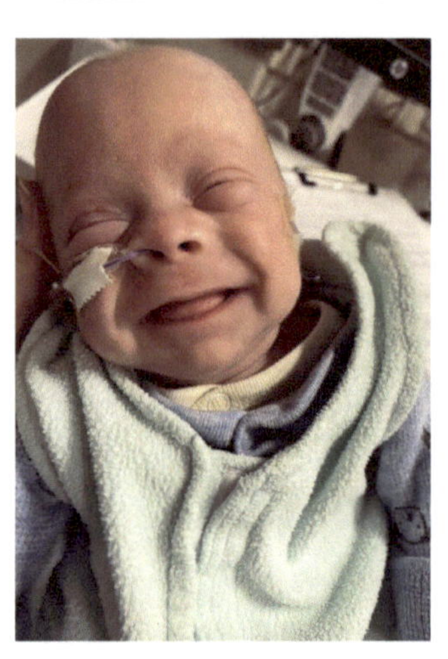

My First
VALENTINE'S
DAY
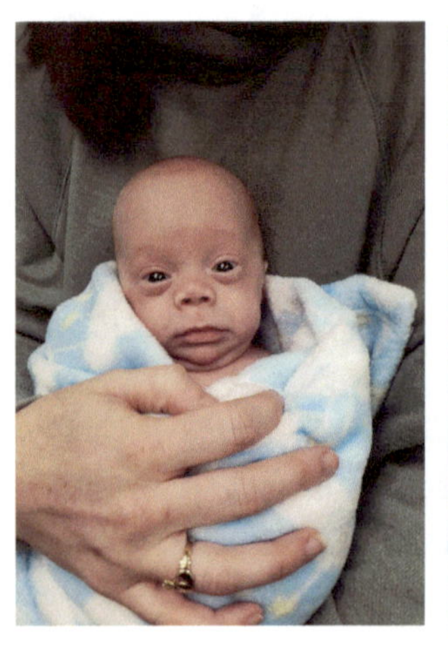
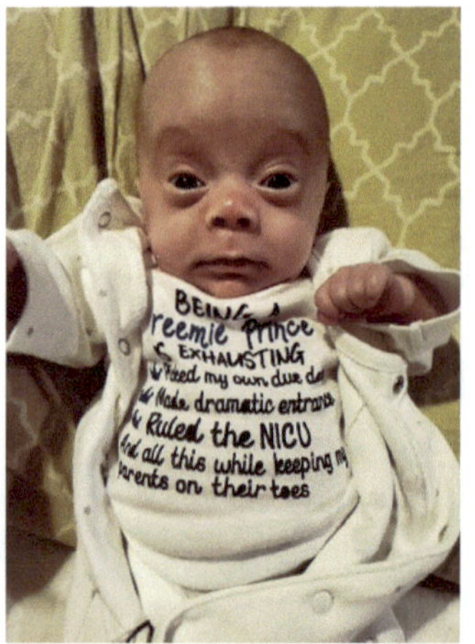
BEING a
reemie Prince
EXHAUSTING
Ruled the NICU
And all this while keeping
rents on their toes
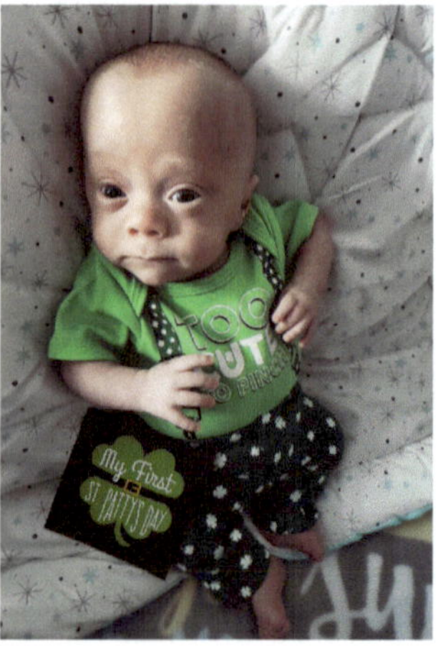
My First
ST PATTY'S DAY

PICTURES NOW

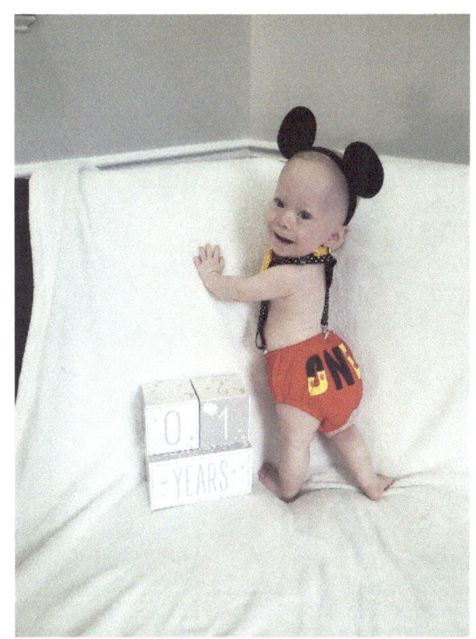

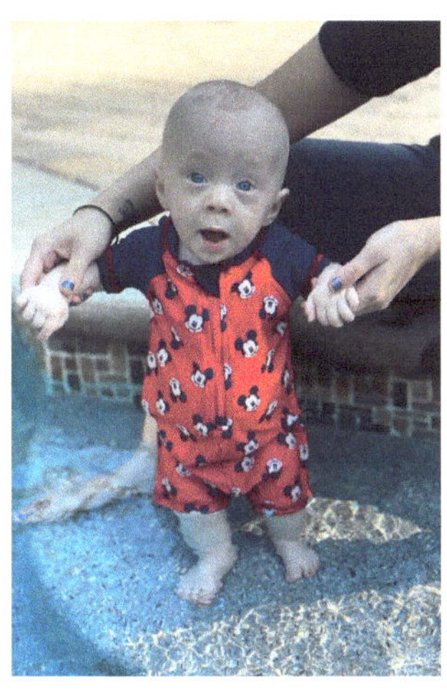

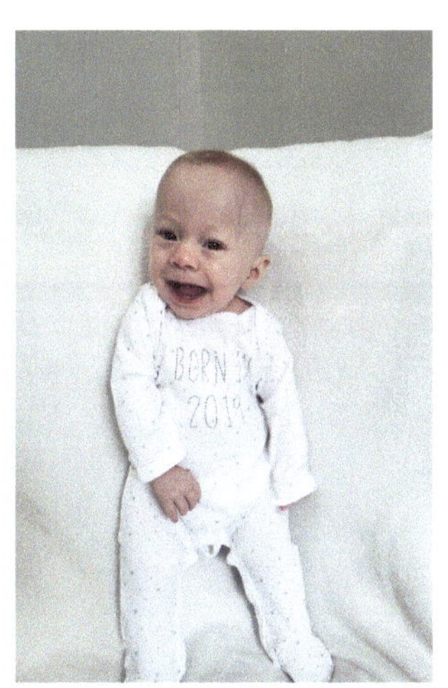

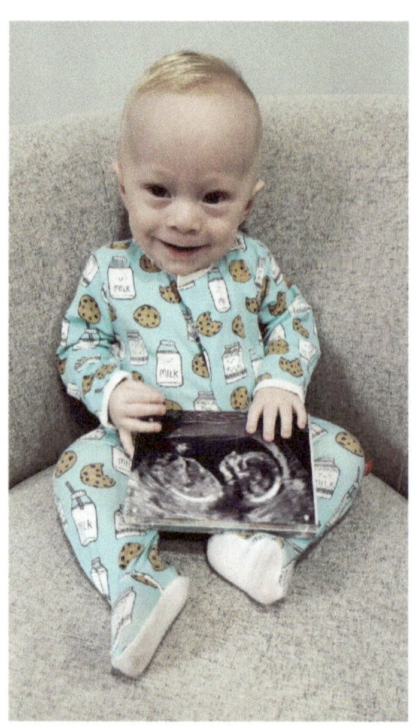

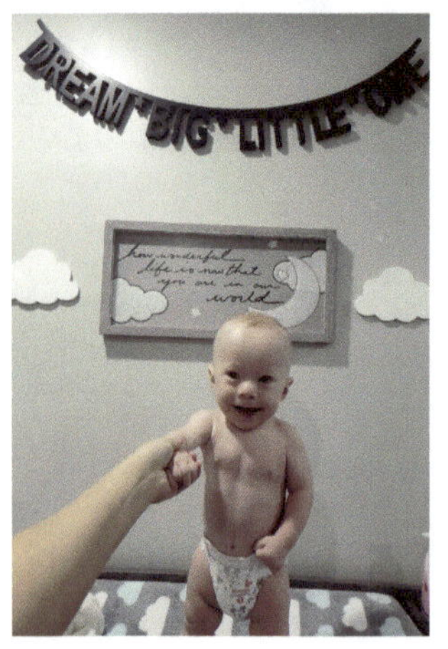

MILESTONES

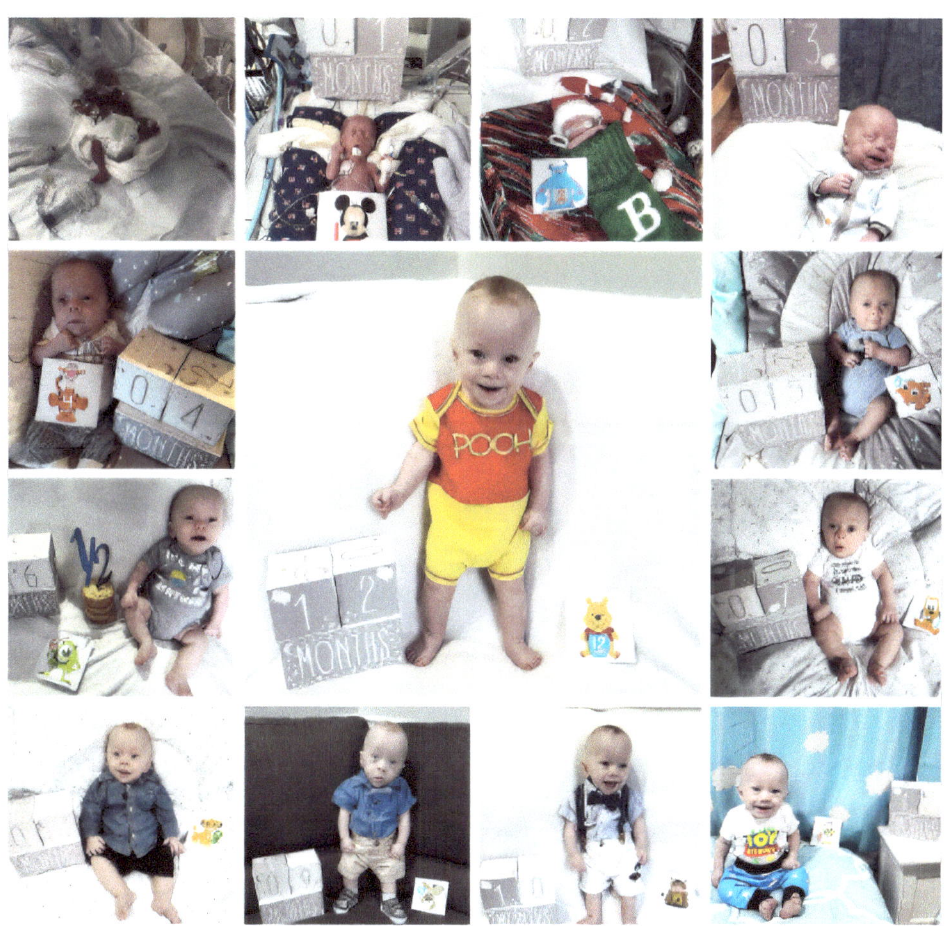